The 13Th Fairy

Kaye Umansky

with illustrations by
Stefano Tambellini

Fife Council Education Department
King's Road Primary School
King's Crescent, Rosyth, KY11 2RS

Barrington Stoke

To Alice and Scarlett

First published in 2014 in Great Britain by
Barrington Stoke Ltd
18 Walker Street, Edinburgh, EH3 7LP

www.barringtonstoke.co.uk

Reprinted 2016

Text © 2014 Kaye Umansky
Illustrations © 2014 Stefano Tambellini

A CIP catalogue record for this book is available
from the British Library upon request

ISBN: 978-1-78112-349-2

Printed in China by Leo

Contents

Chapter 1
Hopping Mad!

Now, let's get one thing clear. I refuse to take the blame. You know what I'm talking about. That business with Sleeping Beauty. I have taken the blame for years and it's time to set the record straight.

Now, I will admit that I went a bit far. You shouldn't mess about with Curses when there are babies around. Curses can go wrong. I know that now. But I do have a bit of a temper. And I was very, *very* cross at the time. More than cross. Hopping mad.

But you would have been upset too.
Imagine your twelve best friends got invited to
a posh party in a palace and you got left out.
How would you feel? Insulted, that's how. Hurt.

Well, I say "twelve best friends", but they're
not my best friends at all. The Twelve Good
Fairies. That's what they call themselves. It's
a sort of club. A club that I'm not in. Not that
I care. I prefer my own company. I can eat
when I want and sleep when I want. Wear the
same socks all week. Leave the washing-up.
Do what I like. You won't catch me being
friends with that lot. I'm not friends with
anyone at all really, but especially not them.

The Twelve Good Fairies wear ballet dresses
and have silly flowery names. They meet in the
woods every Saturday night when the moon is
up. Then they skip around in their soppy fairy
ring, dancing on their tippy-toes and scaring
the squirrels. When they're all puffed out, they
have dewberry tea and fairy cakes, served on
spotty toadstool tables by frogs in bow ties.

That's when they talk about me. I know, because one night I hid behind a bush and listened.

I never get invited to their parties. I wouldn't go anyway. I don't like dancing and pink doesn't suit me. I'm more of a black rags person. I wear a pointy hat. I refuse to have a flowery name. I prefer a broomstick to wings. I'd rather be a witch than a fairy any day. Of course, it wouldn't hurt them to ask me along, just to be polite. But they don't. Just because I'm not like them.

They can keep their stupid old club. I don't care.

Anyway. I was really fed up when I found out that the king and queen had a new baby and the fairies were all invited to the christening! Nobody told me. I only found out when I bumped into Fairy Bluebell at the Post Office. I needed stamps to send off the crossword. I do all the puzzles in the newspaper, every day. I haven't won a prize yet, but you never know.

Bluebell never speaks to me, but that day she was bursting with the news and she couldn't resist showing off.

"Good morning, Grimbleshanks," she trilled. "Tra la la. What a lovely sunny day. I see you're wearing those horrid old black rags again. Don't you find them very hot?"

I could have zapped her there and then, but I didn't want to burn the other people in the Post Office. See how thoughtful I am?

Bluebell waved a big gold envelope under my nose. "I'm here to reply to my invitation! Isn't it too, too exciting?"

"No," I said. "Buying stamps is very, very dull."

"I'm talking about the christening," she said.

"What christening?" I asked.

"The christening at the palace," Bluebell said. "There's a new royal baby. Haven't you heard? Oh, of course you haven't. I forgot. You live all alone and have no friends at all."

"I don't live alone," I told her. "I live with Bill."

Bill is my crow. His full name is Big Bill Beaky. He's lived with me for years.

Perhaps I should tell you how I came to live with Bill.

One snowy morning I went out for some logs and there he was. A big crow, perched on a branch of my apple tree. He had merry little black eyes and a sharp beak. His raggedy feathers were fluffed up against the cold, but he had a cheerful air.

"Cold mornin', ma'am," he said. Very polite, very respectful. And he had this wonderful voice. Not a harsh caw, like most crows. His voice was low, rich and sweet, like honey.

"It is indeed," I said. "Very cold."

"Yep," he said. "Winter's here, for sure. Worms is thin on the ground, I can tell you that."

I asked him in to warm himself by the fire. I made him some toast. We got talking. He told me he was a wandering crow who had travelled for many years in far-off lands and now he was looking to settle down. He said his wings weren't as young as they used to be. What he wanted now was a full belly and a warm fire, that's all.

He has lived with me ever since.

Bill eats bugs, in the main. He likes worms, eggs, frogs and mice for his dinner, too. He's very easy-going about food, although he's not keen on slugs. He says they're over-rated. I always bake him a beetle cake on his birthday. He loves that. He always says, "Aw, shucks. You shouldn't have, Miz Grim." That's the way he talks – in a warm, slow drawl.

Bill doesn't say much, but when he does it's always interesting. Sometimes he sings in his deep, low voice. Most of his songs are about his travels. My favourite one goes like this –

> *"I seen a lotta woe in*
> *the time I been a crow,*
>
> *but I'm livin' in a good*
> *place now."*

I could listen to Bill sing that all night. If he could play guitar, he'd be rich. But he's a crow, so he can't.

But that's enough about Bill. Back to the Post Office and Fairy Bluebell.

"Crows don't count," Bluebell said.

"Bill can count," I snapped. "He can count way past a hundred and add up and take away too, if you must know. And divide and multiply."

Crows are very clever birds. None of the fairies are as clever as Bill. They can't sing, either. Of course, as soon as I'd said how Bill could count, I realised that Bluebell had meant he didn't count *as a friend*. Which was not very nice.

But Bluebell didn't correct me. She wanted to talk about the christening.

"*We're* all going," she said. "We're getting new dresses and we're going to give the baby lovely magical presents, like Love and Joy and Peace. The christening is next Saturday at two o'clock. Are you sure you haven't got an invitation?"

"Must be my new postman," I lied. "He couldn't find the house, I expect. The invite must be delayed."

It wasn't, of course. It had never been sent in the first place. But I didn't want to let Bluebell gloat.

"You'll have to scrub up a bit if you do come," Bluebell said. "But I imagine they've decided not to ask you. It is a *palace*, you know. They have to think of the carpets. Your pointy hat and black rags won't fit in. And that awful, raggedy old bird of yours with his horrid sharp beak wouldn't be welcome. Not with a royal baby about. You'd both be a bit of a downer at a party. Oh, look, here's Primrose! *Coo-eee!* Primrose!"

Fairy Primrose fluttered over. She was clutching another large gold envelope in one hand and a card in the other. The card was covered in glitter and little red hearts and it said in dainty fairy writing –

Dear King and Queen

I would love to come to the christening.
I will bring a very magical gift for your new baby.

Love and kisses from
Fairy Primrose xxx

Fairy Primrose and Fairy Bluebell fell into each other's arms.

"I'm posting my reply to the invitation!" Primrose cried. She was all pink and flustered.

"Me too!" Bluebell squealed. "Isn't it exciting? Everyone's going. Lilac, Rose, Violet, Snowdrop, Pansy, Daisy, Poppy, Daffodil, Holly and Marigold. Everyone except Grimbleshanks. She hasn't had an invitation."

They both stared at me with looks of pity. Well, pretend pity. In fact, they were pleased I wasn't coming. I gave a shrug, to show I didn't care.

"That's because there are only twelve gold plates," Primrose said. "Remember last year, Bluebell, when we went to the palace as guests of honour? When the king and queen got married? There were only twelve gold plates, I'm almost sure of it."

I was thunderstruck. Until now, I hadn't realised I hadn't been invited to the wedding either! Talk about adding insult to injury.

"Twelve gold plates and twelve fairies," Primrose said. "If you were there, there would be thirteen, you see, Grimbleshanks. You'd have to eat from the dog's bowl or something."

They both burst into charming fairy giggles.

"No problem – I'd eat off your gold plate," I said. My face was grim.

"I don't *think* so," said Primrose, and she tossed her curly hair.

"I don't think the plates are the problem," said Bluebell. She stared at me. "The problem is the rags and the pointy hat. And the crow. You don't fit in, Grimbleshanks. You don't have nice, pretty clothes like us. You would lower the tone. Anyway, thirteen's an unlucky number."

"Ah, go and boil your head in an acorn," I said and stomped off in a huff. I didn't bother to buy the stamps. I couldn't care less about the crossword any more. I just wanted to go and kick something.

I could hear them whispering and giggling about me all the way home.

Chapter 2

I Stew for a Week

The whole thing played on my mind. I shouldn't have let it bother me, but it did. I stewed for a whole week. I lost sleep thinking about it. I wondered whether to write a stiff letter of protest to the palace. Then I remembered I didn't have a stamp.

The Good Fairies kept rubbing it in that I didn't have an invite. That didn't help. Little groups of them kept skipping past my gate, chattering about the stupid new frocks they

were going to buy. They made up a mean song.
It went like this –

> *She's not invited to the party,*
> *She's not invited to the party,*
> *She's not invited to the party*
> *And there's nothing she can do!*

Then they'd all fall about laughing. And
sing it again. I didn't find it at all funny.

I kept the curtains closed and pretended I
couldn't hear. But of course I could.

I discussed the matter with Big Bill Beaky.
He always gives me good advice.

"Bill," I said. "I can't stand this."

"Let it go, Miz Grim. Let it go," Bill said
from his perch. "They'll get tired of teasin'
you."

"I can't," I said. "I need to do something.
It's really getting to me."

"Write a nice letter to the palace, then," Bill said. "Ask them to send you an invite."

"I haven't got a stamp," I huffed. "Anyway, it's too late to be nice now. I need to do something big and dramatic. I'm angry, Bill. I need to get it out of my system. Only then can I move on."

"Forget it, Miz Grim. Nothin' good ever comes of gettin' all riled up," Bill said.

"I'm not thinking 'Good'. I'm thinking 'Bad'."

"Ain't good for you," said Bill. "Thinkin' 'Bad'."

"I don't care," I said. "I'm thinking about a Curse."

"A Curse," said Bill. He gave a little whistle, put his head on one side and stared at me. "Hm. That's kinda strong, ain't it?"

He was right. But I didn't want to let it go.
I'm good at Curses. Curses are my style. I can
Curse louder than anyone I know, and I can
magic up a nice bit of thunder and lightning to
go with it.

"They won't forget a Curse in a hurry," I
said.

In my mind, I could see myself in the great
hall at the palace. I would wave my wand about
while everyone shivered in their socks. I would
deliver a Curse that would knock the spots off
the Good Fairies' soppy gifts.

"Who you gonna Curse?" Bill asked.

"Well ..." I said. "The baby, I suppose."

"Why the baby? What's the baby done?"

I couldn't answer that. The baby had done
nothing.

"You sure 'bout this?" asked Bill. "I mean, I know you're angry an' all that. But ain't it a bit over the top to curse the baby?"

"It'll be fine," I said. "Don't worry, I'll plan it properly. I've got to make sure I get the words right. I won't *really* hurt the baby. I'll just shake them all up a bit. Show the Good Fairies some real magic. Teach the king and queen a lesson about good manners. Show them what happens when they upset me. Don't argue, Bill. I've made up my mind."

"OK, then." Bill shrugged his wings and sighed. "If that's the way you wanna play it."

"It is," I said.

"Just make sure you get them words right."

"I will. Ready for your worms now?"

"Yup," said Bill. "Bring 'em on."

He's always ready for his worms.

Chapter 3
Pulling out the Stops

So that's why I steamed into the palace like I did, on the day of the christening. I had it all worked out. I knew exactly the message I wanted to get across. I had learned the words of the Curse off by heart. I had my wand. My temper was up. I was ready.

That morning, Bill had said he would come with me for moral support.

"You don't have to," I said. "I know you think this is a bad idea."

"Hey," said Bill. "I've still got your back. You an' me's buddies, right?"

Bill's good like that. Very loyal. I took him in out of the cold and he says he won't forget that. Even when I'm being unreasonable, which I am sometimes.

And so I screeched across the sky on my broomstick to the palace. Bill rode on my arm to save his wings. It's a fair old way and he's getting on a bit now. He says his travellin' days are over.

I flew down over the palace gardens. The broom's not as accurate as it once was, and I had to make an emergency stop. I landed on my bottom in a rose bush, which put me in a vile mood. I was scratched and pricked all over by thorns.

"You OK, Miz Grim?" Bill asked as he zig-zagged down.

"I'm fine," I said, as I picked the thorns out of my bum. I had a nasty scratch on my chin too.

"You sure?" Bill said. "Cos we can go on home and get you a cup of tea and a plaster."

"Not a chance," I said. "Come on. We've got a Curse to do."

Bill hopped up onto my arm and I stood up. I took my wand out and checked that it was working. I gave it a little shake and green sparks fizzed out, like they're supposed to. Then Bill and I marched up to the palace.

The guards on the door saw the look on my face and my fizzing wand. They didn't dare try to stop me.

But when I'd got past them, there was a snooty footman at the door asking for the golden invitations. He had a big pile of them on a small table. He asked me for mine. I laughed in his face, kicked the table over and stormed in.

They were all in there in the big hall. King, queen, baby, celebrities, courtiers, reporters, guests, you name it. The palace staff had pulled out all the stops. There were balloons and fancy nibbles and a great big pink and white cake. Above all their heads there was a huge banner that said –

WELCOME, PRINCESS BEAUTY

When I barged in, the Twelve Good Fairies were crowded round a frilly crib with their soppy gifts for the baby.

The baby was a nice little thing, actually. I could see that. She lay in her cradle and smiled and cooed at everyone. She didn't seem to mind being given Happiness and Wisdom and Health and whatnot, although I suspect she would have been just as happy with some mashed banana. Maybe I would magic some up for her later.

But first, I had a Curse to deliver.

Chapter 4

The Curse

Now, the Curse.

I'm going to have to explain this carefully.
A lot of people think I said something I didn't.
They think I said, "*On her 16th birthday she
will prick her finger on a spindle **and die**.*" But
I didn't. I never said anything about dying.
What I was *going* to say was, "*She will prick her
finger on a spindle **and I** will give her a sticking
plaster.*"

But I never got to say it. I had my wand out and the thunder was thundering nicely. I got as far as, "*On her 16th birthday she will prick her finger on a spindle **and I** ...*"

Say it out loud and you'll see the problem.

And then everyone started to scream and rush about and I didn't get to say the last words. Which were pretty important. But it's hard to speak when the Captain of the Guard has got you in a headlock.

You're surprised to hear the truth, eh? I thought you would be. But you shouldn't believe those nasty rumours people like to spread about me. It's important to listen to both sides of a story.

I promise you, all I ever meant to do was to wait until the princess was older, then lure her into a quiet attic where no one would disturb us. Then she would prick her finger – nothing *too* bad, but there does have to be at least a

tiny bit of nastiness, or else a Curse is not a Curse.

But then I would give the princess a plaster to show her how nice and helpful I can be. We would have a long chat and I would tell her about how mean everyone was to me 16 years ago, when she was christened.

I would tell her about the Good Fairy club, and about how I didn't get invited to anything, ever. I would explain about the Curse and how it was a protest at how unfair it all was, but how it was nothing personal and I never meant any real harm. The princess would see things from my point of view and she would be sure not to repeat the mistakes of her rude parents. We would become firm friends. She would invite me as guest of honour to her 16th birthday party.

But then everyone heard me wrong.

And, as a result, I was marched out by the Captain of the Guard, who still had me bent over in a headlock. Bill dive-bombed him again and again from above, but the Captain of the Guard just batted him away. Bill didn't even get a peck in. He did his best, but he's not a pecker by nature. He lost quite a lot of feathers.

Chapter 5
A Thousand Times Worse

Bill and I went home to nurse our wounds.

If the king and queen were going to be like that, I would let them think the worst. Think of all the trouble they were going to have for the next 16 years. They would have to ban spinning wheels all over the kingdom. It wouldn't make them very popular. They would probably ban pins and needles too, just to be on the safe side.

"Just wait until people's pants start falling down," I said to Bill. "When the elastic goes there'll be no safety pins to keep them up. There'll be an outcry."

"I guess," said Bill.

"Wait until their clothes are all ragged and they can't make any new ones," I said. "The Good Fairies won't be able to buy any new dresses for their dances."

"Think of that," said Bill. "No shoppin' trips for clothes. What a world."

I think he was being sarcastic.

"OK, so it's not much of a revenge for what they did to me," I said, "but it's better than nothing."

"Hmm," said Bill.

"Anyway, it's only for 16 years," I said. "Then I can make it all right and get to move in royal circles again."

"That what you wanna do?" Bill asked.

"Well, I'd like to have the chance," I said. "Think how jealous the Fairies will be when I'm best friends with the princess."

At that point, I hadn't realised that something unexpected had happened.

It was that silly little Fairy Violet who really messed things up. She got in on the act and made things a thousand times worse. After I'd been marched out the hall, she still had her gift to give, you see. She decided to be clever and soften the Curse. The rules of magic let you have one go at doing that.

And so Fairy Violet changed my harmless "*and I*" bit to "*and fall asleep for a hundred years*". What a pest.

I know this because she came round and told me so. In fact, that night, all of the Fairies came round in an angry, fluttering mob. I didn't invite them in, of course. They stood and

shouted through the letterbox. They wanted to tell me what a disgrace I was. I ignored them until they went away.

If only Violet hadn't meddled. Princess Beauty would have pricked her finger, we would have had our cosy little chat and the whole thing would have ended there. But, no. Violet thought she knew best.

There was nothing I could do about it. The Curse was now well and truly cast, with Violet's bit of nonsense tagged on.

In 16 years, the princess could have had a plaster on her finger and me as a new best friend. But now the poor girl would be stuck with falling asleep for a hundred years. I had to go along with it. You can't mess about with the power of a Curse.

Chapter 6

Spinning Wheels and Broomsticks

You may wonder what happened over the next 16 years. Well, not a lot at first. I kept my head down. As you can imagine, I wasn't popular – what with all the trousers that were falling down and clothes that were falling apart at the seams since nobody was allowed to do any spinning or sewing or whatnot.

The Good Fairies were always coming round to throw eggs at my door. Bill enjoyed eating the eggs. The fairies' dresses were beginning to look quite shabby. I never went out to confront them. I just stayed in and only ever took my broomstick out at night, when there was no one around to shout "Boo!" at me.

It's boring, never going out. I found myself twiddling my thumbs with nothing to do. Bill made me buy a guitar, so I could play while he sang. It was funny, but I found I had a knack. I picked it up in no time. We spent some great musical evenings by the fire, me strumming away on the guitar while I learned Bill's songs. There were a lot of them. Most were about lonely flying and worm shortages.

I had a lot of time to think, too. All right, so it wasn't my fault that Princess Beauty was doomed to fall asleep for a hundred years. But it wouldn't have happened if I hadn't messed about with Curses in the first place. Bill didn't say "I told you so", which was good of him. I really should have listened to him. But it was too late now.

So there I was, 16 years later, up in the palace attic with my spinning wheel.

I peddled away like an expert, although I can't say I was having fun. It was a wet night and I would rather have stayed at home. Balancing a spinning wheel on a broomstick in the rain is no joke. I had a wet crow huddled up against me, too. But you have to show up when Curses are involved. It's in the rules.

Bill was perched on a rafter, drying out and singing a song called "Slug Blues". It goes like this –

> *"Woke up this mornin' hopin'*
> *for some bugs,*
>
> *early bird had got 'em an' all*
> *that's left is slugs."*

His warm, bass tones calmed me down a bit. I was glad to have him there. I was nervous. I needed my plans to go right.

Downstairs, everyone was busy getting ready for the birthday party. It hadn't started yet. The kitchen was in uproar. The king and queen were wrapping up presents in the throne room. Servants were blowing up balloons and polishing golden plates. No one had any time for the birthday girl.

So, Beauty was bored and wandered up to the attic, just like she was supposed to do. It was the Curse that made her, of course. *"She will prick her finger on a spindle."* That's what I had said. I wish I hadn't. If I'd kept my big mouth shut, I could have been home by the fire with a cup of cocoa and my guitar.

"Hello," said Beauty, sticking her pretty head around the door. She didn't sound a bit scared – just curious. "Who are you, please?" she asked.

'What a polite young woman,' I thought.

"My name's Grimbleshanks, dear," I said. "Come on in." I did my best to smile like a harmless old lady.

"What are you doing, please?" she asked.

"Spinning," I said.

"Spinning," said Beauty. "Is that what you call it?"

"Why, yes," I said. "Haven't you ever seen a spinning wheel before, my dear?"

"No," she said. "Is spinning difficult? Can you show me how, please?"

"Oh no, my pretty one, it's not hard. It's easy. Do you want to try?"

Well, you know what happened next. I showed her how the spinning wheel worked, then she pricked her finger on the spindle, fell into a pile of wool and nodded off. Fast asleep she was, right there on the spot.

"That's it, then, Miz Grim," Bill said from his perch. "You done your bit."

"Yes," I said. "I have."

"Happy now?" said Bill.

I didn't say anything. I picked up a blanket I'd brought with me. I spread it over Beauty and tucked her in.

"Sorry, love," I whispered. "Not my doing." But she was fast asleep and didn't hear me.

Chapter 7
Revenge Isn't Sweet

The Curse took effect straight away.

At the same time as Beauty pricked her finger, everyone else in the palace fell asleep. I didn't expect that. It wasn't in my Curse, or in the bit that busybody Violet added on either. But that's the trouble with Curses. There can be unexpected side-effects.

Bill and I went down and had a look around. They were all frozen where they were.

The king and queen slept on their thrones in the great hall. In the kitchen, the cook was fast asleep with her hand raised to box the pot-boy's ears. I snapped my fingers under their noses and they didn't stir. It was spooky.

I stuck a pin in the Captain of the Guard – the one who'd had me in a headlock. Sadly, he didn't feel it.

"You can peck him if you like," I said to Bill.

"Nah," he said. "I ain't one for bearin' grudges."

We didn't hang about after that. Revenge wasn't sweet. Not at all. Beauty was a nice little thing. She didn't deserve this. Nobody did. Not even the Captain of the Guard.

I packed up the spinning wheel and we flew home. I had a strong cup of tea with four sugars, which usually makes me feel better. This time, it didn't.

Bill told me not to fret.

"What's done is done," he said. "It was a mistake, right? Don't beat yourself up."

I did, though. A hundred years is a long time to be asleep. Even if it wasn't my fault. Well, not quite my fault. Like I said, it wouldn't have happened if I'd kept my temper in check and shown a bit more self-control.

Oh, well. There was nothing to do now but wait it out.

In ten years, so many trees had grown up around the palace that you couldn't see it from the road.

I suppose I could have popped in and checked on what was happening inside, but I never felt like it. Anyway, I knew what was happening. The spiders would be spinning their webs and the dust would be gathering. There was nothing I could do about it. Why would I go there, just to stand around and crow? Crowing wouldn't help. Bill didn't want to crow either, and he *is* one – a crow, I mean.

Twenty years later, I'd got pretty good on guitar. Bill said I should buy a saxophone.

Thirty years later, I'd mastered the sax and moved on to the clarinet. Life wasn't so bad. People were using pins and needles and spinning again. After all, the Curse had happened, so there wasn't any point in keeping the ban going.

Forty years on, everyone seemed to have forgotten the whole business. People nodded to me in the Post Office and commented on the nice music they heard coming from my cottage.

Not the Twelve Good Fairies, mind. They hadn't forgotten. They always crossed the road when they saw me coming.

More years passed. Bill and I were asked to perform a little concert at the village hall.

It went down rather well. We had a packed house.

The Fairies didn't come.

Chapter 8
A Kiss, of all Things

So. A hundred years have gone by. A hundred years of Good Fairy dances, and I haven't been invited to any of them. Who cares? I don't need friends like them.

I've mellowed a lot. Well, a hundred years is a long time. We're all older and wiser now. I'm not so grumpy these days. I've made friends with a couple of local witches (Mrs Offal and Mrs Tripe) and a Wise Woman called Mrs Gumption. They wear black rags too.

I met Mrs Offal first, in the butcher's. She said she'd heard that I had a crow with a fine singing voice. She told me that she played the accordion.

"Really? You should bring it round one night," I said.

"I'd love to, Grimbleshanks," she said. "Tonight OK?"

That was a first! Me inviting a visitor round! I wasn't sure after I'd done it, but Bill said it was a great idea. We both cleared the place up, and I made some cakes and put a clean cloth on the table. I felt a bit nervous.

I needn't have. Mrs Offal came round and we had a fine old time. She said she had a friend who played the spoons (Mrs Tripe) and Mrs Tripe knew of a Wise Woman who played bassoon.

So now we've got a proper sort of group going. Bill sings, of course. We call ourselves

the Big Bill Beaky Band. We practise every Thursday. We drink a lot of tea.

They bring sponge cake to share, and a selection of bugs for Bill.

Anyway. Tonight's the night. The Curse will end and I hope there will be a happy ending. I hope. But I'm not so sure.

Violet can never leave things alone. She just had to be the clever one who softened the Curse and then, would you believe, she added yet more stuff. A lot of extra details about a handsome prince who would wake Beauty with a *kiss*, of all things.

Nobody told me this to my face. I heard it from Mrs Tripe, who heard it from someone in the Post Office. For goodness' sake. I wish she'd stop dabbling. Violet, I mean. Why add a prince to make life difficult? Bill agrees. He thinks Beauty should enjoy herself before she settles down. He thinks 116 is way too young to get married.

I'm not a great fan of kissing either. Isn't it better to be woken by an alarm clock? Who'd want to be kissed before they'd brushed the cobwebs off and cleaned their teeth? A lot of dirt will have built up in a hundred years. It's a long time to go without a wash.

But maybe Beauty won't mind. After all, the prince will be handsome. That's a start.

Imagine sleeping for a hundred years. I bet she's ready for her breakfast.

Perhaps there will be another royal wedding before long.

They'd better invite me.

Or else.

♫ The Big Bill Beaky Band ♪♪

Bill	Lead singer
Grimbleshanks	Guitar, saxophone and clarinet
Mrs Offal	Accordion
Mrs Tripe	Spoons
Mrs Gumption	Bassoon

BILL: *Ain't no good to lose your temper (strum, strum).*

Temper, temper (toot toot, wheeze).

No, it ain't no good to lose your temper (clink, clank, warble, strum).

If you aimin' for a happy life,

Oh yeaaaaaahh.

US: *Strum, toot, warble, clink, clank, wheeze, strum.*

Our books are tested
for children and young people by
children and young people.

Thanks to everyone who consulted on
a manuscript for their time and effort in
helping us to make our books better
for our readers.